Loving His Darkness
By
Simone Black
Carnal Nature Series

This is a work of fiction. Similarities to real people, places, or events are entirely coincidental.

LOVING HIS DARKNESS

First edition. October 25, 2021.

Copyright © 2021 Simone Black.

Written by Simone Black.

This book contains themes of captivity and violence that may be too much for some readers. There are some very bad men in this book. But at least one of them is ready to take care of the heroine and help her survive the night...

There is a happy ever after. That's my promise to you. Thank you for choosing to read Loving His Darkness.

Ivy

I should have started running much sooner.

My head feels like it's spinning, and I think I'm gonna fall over. I look behind me and notice that he's still following me—the large man who appears to be lumbering towards me like a monster out of a slasher movie.

Falling down onto the pavement, I hear my short red dress rip. It was more than a little too tight to begin with, and if it wasn't part of my "slutty Halloween" costume, I never would have worn it.

I rake my fingers through my hair. "Shit," I whisper. Scrambling back onto my feet is a real process. It just doesn't seem possible as I keep falling back down. My heart pounds harder than a freight train, and I take quick shallow breaths.

"I just want to talk to you," a gruff voice calls out.

"Fat chance of that!" I shout back.

I know he's lying. Of course, he doesn't want to just talk to me. If I don't keep trying to get away, this will most likely be it for me. My mind whirs with the consequences of that as I struggle to get back up. Once my feet are firm on the ground again, I pull my heels off, throw them into the grass, and take off running as fast as I can. Those weren't my favorite shoes or anything, anyway. They were just bought for this naughty little costume my best friend talked me into. I wore it, because she said I looked hot, and might find a boyfriend at the party. No—I don't want a boyfriend right now. There's too much going on in my life, and my father's life, that I would have no time for a relationship. But

Tara had been insistent, so I wore the dress and heels to pacify her.

Now I felt like killing her—for this as well as the fact that she abandoned me with no way home. She met a new guy, and as always, ran off somewhere with him never to be seen for the rest of the night. Typical Tara, yet I kept putting up with it, and usually just calling myself an Uber. But this time my phone died because I forgot to charge it before I left the party, and I just figured I could walk home anyway. It was only two miles, right? That's nothing...

"I just want to talk to you, Ivy!" the man shouts.

Shit. How does he know my name? There's no time to figure that out right now, and I'm not gonna stop to talk to him and ask either. So, I just keep running, just focusing on the dark road ahead of me, as my bare feet hit the rough pavement.

It feels like the ground is gonna give way beneath me as I hear someone running behind me. He's decided the walk slow horror movie method isn't gonna work on me. I'm grateful I ran track in high school, and even more grateful that I was good at it. But it's been a few years, and my lungs just can't take what they used to. Just a few more feet and I'll probably collapse.

He grabs my arm and yanks me towards him.

"Trust me," he says. "I don't want to do this to you. I have to."

I scream and he clamps his hand over my mouth. The rough callouses on his hand scrape against my skin. He must work with his hands a lot. He has a manly smell about him, and even though he's holding me hostage in this moment, my womanhood betrays me, and I feel a slight trickle of wetness between my legs.

Kicking his knees and flailing about while screaming does nothing to my captor. He's powerful, immovable, immensely dangerous.

"Stop struggling, and I promise this will go much easier for you," he says. "I promise you I'm not gonna hurt you. We just need to talk to you."

I give up and let himself go limp in his arms. He pulls me in tighter against his hard body, and I feel something poking against my back. He's getting off on this.

The beast of a man slings me over his shoulder, and I resume kicking, and struggling. But it still does nothing, and no one at all comes to my aid.

He carries me to a car where I'm thrown into a trunk, and the lid is slammed hard. I keep screaming hoping that someone will notice or care. There has to be someone out right now who would be willing to help me.

The car starts, and soon we're speeding down the road. I'm tossed about in the trunk, and it seems like this street has more potholes than any other. The bumps make my stomach lurch.

Eventually, we stop, but I'm not released from the trunk. I think my brain is shutting down. There's a fog taking over my mind, and all I can think is that this is where I die at the age of 21—secret daughter of Chicago's new mayor, and good girl virgin. Though the good girl part is questionable in my current outfit, or at least it will be in the police report, I'm sure.

My captor gets out of the car, and slams the door shut. Then he opens the trunk and picks me up. He tosses me in the back, and I land with a thud on the leather seats.

I look around. This is definitely not a nice neighborhood. It's a bit run down, and I see several men hanging around outside the car. One of them points at me, and laughs.

I try the doors, and they're all child locked. Shit. I lie down and kick the windows, hoping to break them and escape. But it's no use—I'm too weak—too small. Not as tough as I thought I was.

"Let me out of this car, you bastards!" I shout.

As if that will somehow get the response I'm hoping for—that one of them will take pity on me and set me free.

"I did what you asked and got you the girl," my captor says to another man.

The street is dark, and my eyes are fogging over, so I can't get a good look at any of these men. I have no idea how many there are, or if they have weapons.

"You did exactly what you said you'd do, as always, Raptor," a man says. His voice is emotionless, and the sound of it sends a ripple of ice across my skin.

I swallow hard and try to think—try to regain my full mental strength. All I can think of though is that Raptor must be the name of the guy who took me. It's kind of ridiculous, but I'm sure it's his gang name and not the one his mother gave him.

"Good work on grabbing the little slut," another icy calm voice says.

"Just pay me the money and I'll give you the girl," Raptor replies.

Laughter booms in my ears.

"Do you really think it's going to be that easy? You owe us—a lot. And that means you're coming with us to guard the girl and make sure she doesn't try anything that will get her killed before the right time."

Killed before the right time. Those are the words my brain focuses on. I whisper to myself, "Ok, Ivy. You can cry now." Tears come on cue and slide down my cheeks. I bury my face in my hands and sob. I'm giving up much too easy, but I'm not sure there's a whole lot of options anyway. My situation feels pretty damn hopeless.

Something thuds against the car—probably a body. "Pay me, or I'll kill both of you now," Raptor growls. "And then I'll keep the ransom money for myself."

Ransom. So that's what they're planning to do with me. Makes sense. They found out about me—the secret my father was trying to keep his entire life. He kept me a secret, but paid for everything, and took care of me and my mom for as long as we promised not to say a word. He didn't give us much, but he gave us just enough to live a normal life. He said he didn't want me to grow up a spoiled brat or anything. To hell with him though, and to hell with all of these men.

"You wouldn't do a thing, unless you want Griffon to have you killed. You might think you're a tough guy Navy Seal or whatever, but you wouldn't last five minutes if Griffon wanted you dead. Now come on and drag the girl out of the car. The longer we wait out here, the more witnesses we'll have to kill," the original icy voiced man says.

The car door is opened, and Raptor drags me out of it. Once again, I'm kicking and screaming as he flings me over his massive hard shoulder and carries me off. The other men laugh as we go inside a dark building. Raptor carries me down several flights of stairs in a dimly lit stairwell. I cry the entire time.

"Shut up, girl. Please just cooperate and we'll be able to do this as smoothly as possible."

"Cooperate in what?" I ask. "My own death?"

"That's not gonna happen, sweetheart," he says.

My cheeks burn hot as he says the word "sweetheart". No man has ever called me that before, certainly not my father. I've had a total of zero boyfriends, because I've never been a popular girl, and that's exactly how I like it. It lets me live a quiet life where no one bothers me, because other than my mom, and a few friends, I haven't let anyone get close enough to me to bother me. I like feeling like a secret.

Raptor sets me down in a chair, and someone else chains me to it. They bind my hands, and feet. Then pull a pillowcase over my head and tie it around my neck. I cough as it becomes hard to breathe. Someone kicks the chair from behind, and I lurch forward onto the ground, scraping my knees against the cement.

"Fucking asshole," Raptor says. "If you want my help, you're not allowed to hurt her, Lorenzo. You got that?"

"Oh, I'm shaking so hard right now," Lorenzo replies.

"Let me take the pillowcase off, and I'll tie it around her eyes instead. She just needs a blindfold. You don't have to cut off her air."

Raptor is so considerate of my well-being. If he hadn't kidnapped me, I might think he liked me.

"We have business to take care of anyhow. Do whatever you want with her, as long as you don't spoil her little pussy. That's for us later tonight," Lorenzo says.

"What's going to happen to me?" I ask.

"You'll be fine. Just stay put until we're done, and then you can go home," Raptor says.

I wonder why he's protecting me.

"You're a good liar, Raptor," Lorenzo says.

I burst into tears and find myself being picked up off the ground and sat back in the chair.

It was naive of me to even consider for a second that Raptor was protecting me. I let myself feel a shred of hope, and now's it's stamped out, just as I should have known it would be.

"We'll see you later, girlie," Lorenzo says.

I hear the other two men leaving the room—their heavy footsteps pounding the cement. A door slams shut.

Raptor removes my pillowcase. I look around the dark room, and my eyes just can't seem to come into focus. I'm not sure what's wrong with me. It's probably just because I'm so upset, and my eyes are full of tears. If I can just calm myself down, I might be able to think and figure a way out of this.

Raptor slides a finger under my chin and tilts my face up towards his.

"I'm telling you, Ivy. If you don't make any trouble, you'll get out of this just fine. I'm gonna make sure of it."

I spit on him, and he laughs as he wipes it away.

"Go to hell. You're nothing but a liar," I snarl.

"I know there's no way you can think any differently of me, so I won't try to change your mind. But if you're at all worried about those other two guys hurting you, I promise I'll kill them before they even have a chance. Got it?"

So, he is trying to help me—in his own way anyway. I mean, if he really wanted to help me, he wouldn't have kidnapped me to begin with.

He leaves me sitting in the chair and turns on a small lamp. It's not much light, but it's enough for me to finally see him at last. He pulls a chair a few feet from mine and stares at me.

He's big, alright. I heard the other guy say he was a Navy Seal, so it makes sense. Raptor's got on a tight black t-shirt that makes no attempt at hiding his muscles. His arms are covered in tattoos, and I'm willing to bet the rest of him is too. I wonder what they all mean to him. He's wearing tight jeans, and I can tell by the bulge in them that he's packing something huge.

I look up and fix my eyes on his face. He's handsome and rugged and has a strong jaw and piercing blue eyes. The most striking thing though, is the scar running down the left side of his face. It starts at the corner of his eye and continues all the way to the edge of his mouth. I can't imagine how bad whatever it was must have been to leave such a mark.

"Are you ready to cooperate, sweetheart?" he asks.

"No," I answer. "What are your friends trying to do with me?"

"Just sit there quietly, and don't make any trouble. I don't want to put the blindfold on you, but I'll do it if you sit there jabbering away the whole time. I won't just blindfold you, but I'll shove a rag in your mouth and tape it over. This is for you own good."

Maybe snark is what I need to combat him, since I don't have the strength to break free and take him on.

"Sounds kinky," I say. I force myself to smile, and he chuckles.

"Yeah, well, I've always been a bit of a freak," he says.

"Why did you kidnap me?" I ask.

"I told you. We have business to take care of. I thought you knew that already."

"But you didn't explain it to me."

"We know who you are, Ivy. And those other guys need a few favors from your father. That's all."

"And what do you need?"

He runs his fingers through his short dark hair, turns away from me, and coughs.

"You don't need to worry about that right now," he says. "Just know that I'm here to protect you."

"Bullshit," I whisper.

Raptor turns back towards me, and I bite my bottom lip as I stare at his mouth, and the bottom of his scar. No doubt he's seen some horrible things in his life, and maybe he doesn't want to see them again. Maybe I can trust him. But can I trust myself around him?

That's something I'm not too sure about. If circumstances were different, I'd want him to kiss me.

Raptor

Ivy Rose Walker is one hell of a girl. And the only thing staring at her all night is gonna do is get me into more trouble than I'm already in. Still, I can't help myself. Her soft, smooth cheeks have a hint of blush, and the few freckles she has just add to her perfect innocence. I've been following Ivy for a week now, waiting for the right moment to take her—wondering if I should even go through with it. So, I know she doesn't normally wear a too short dress like this one. I also know she doesn't usually look so vulnerable. Innocent—yes. Vulnerable—no.

She's a small girl, and I'd break her in half if I ever tried to climb on top of her, but damn, she's got a body to die for. My dick twitches in my pants again. Since the first moment I saw Ivy Walker a week ago, I've been unable to keep the thing down.

"Why don't you just untie me?" she asks. "I'll let you do whatever you want to me if you untie me."

She bats her long eyelashes at me.

"I don't want you," I lie. "You're not my type."

Usually, no one is my type. Since I came home from the navy, I haven't laid a hand on a woman until I touched Ivy tonight. I knew that I'd end up getting too close to them, and they'd find themselves in trouble for it somehow. Trouble follows me everywhere no matter what I try to do to shake it off.

I'm not the kind of man a woman can take home to her mother. Not with everything I've seen forever haunting me no matter where I go. I know what I am. I'm a monster. I've killed people, and I've done it on purpose. I can't deny it anymore. I'm a killer. I've been a Navy Seal for years, and I know how to kill with deadly precision.

But I don't want to be a murderer. I just want to live my life without fear of being found out.

"You're not a killer, Raptor," Ivy says. It's like she can read my mind.

I shake my head and grind my teeth. She'll try everything she can to break me and get me to set her free. And though I want to more than anything, I just can't do it.

But the reason why isn't as obvious as it might seem.

She runs her tongue along her bottom lip. "Can I at least have some water?"

"Haven't got any water here, sweetheart. And I can't leave to get you any either."

"Can't you tell those other guys to bring it?"

"No," I reply.

She hangs her head. "My dad's not gonna cooperate with you guys. If he does, everyone will find out about me. I'll be in the news and his career will be ruined."

I can't imagine anyone thinking they'd be ruined by someone knowing Ivy was theirs—whether she be their daughter or their lover.

"If he doesn't cooperate, my associates will try to kill you. But your father will cooperate. You're not the only thing those guys have on him."

"Oh," she whispers.

"You're nothing but a bonus check in their eyes." I'm lying to her, but she doesn't need to know that. She is the only thing they've got on her father. The bastard is mostly too clean for a politician. It's suspicious, for sure. Ivy is his one deep, dark secret. But I have to make her think he'll pay the ransom. She needs hope right now, and it's the only thing I can really give her.

The door swings open, and I look over to see Lorenzo and Terrence are back. They walk in with several bags of stuff. They join me and Ivy and set their bags down beside her.

"I figured you'd be hungry, slut," Lorenzo says. "So, I thought I'd get you something. Wouldn't want you to starve."

He pulls a candy bar out of the bag, unwraps it, and holds it out for Ivy. Of course, her hands are chained, and she can't take it. The bastard laughs.

"Oh, that's right," he says. "Guess you'll just have to watch us eat then."

He takes a bite out of the candy bar, and I leap out of my chair. Grabbing the gun at my side, I shove the barrel up against the back of Lorenzo's head.

Terrence just laughs and pulls a bag of chips out of the grocery bag. He tears it open and crunches as loud as he can—I'm sure to torture Ivy.

"You would never shoot me, Raptor. Because you're not a stupid man," Lorenzo says.

"You don't know what I'll do or won't do," I growl. "Now give the girl something to eat. "

He holds his candy bar close to her mouth.

"No thanks," she says. "Not after you put your dirty mouth on it."

I keep my eyes on Terrence as he crosses the room. He returns with the ball gag we stashed earlier before we brought Ivy here.

"We'll all be much happier if she can't talk," Terrence says as he tries to force the ball gag into Ivy's mouth. She fights him like a champion, keeping her mouth shut tight, and refusing to take it. But he pries her mouth open and shoves it in. He straps it, tightens it, and looks over his work.

Now would be the perfect time to shoot them both, take the girl, and run. At this point though, I don't think I'd set her free either. I'd take her with me somewhere far away from here, rip that dress off, and fuck her till she calls me daddy. Then of course, I'd marry her, and get to work making babies so we could be a family. Yeah, sometimes I can be a sensitive guy, and Ivy brings that out in me.

But life is too complicated right now for all that, and I pull my gun away from Lorenzo's head, and sit back down with the gun now resting in my lap. I watch the tears fall from Ivy's face as she tries to speak through the gag.

This building is loaded with Griffon's men right now, and there's no way I can shoot these two, and expect to get away with it for long. And if I die, Ivy dies with me. I know it, so I can't risk it no matter how long I have to watch her cry.

"You're a good man, Raptor," Lorenzo says. "But if you put a gun to my head ever again, you better be ready to fire it."

"Deal," I reply.

"We're heading out again to go to talk to the boss. We just wanted to see how you two were getting along. Don't take the damn gag out of her mouth though. You were supposed to blindfold her, gag her, and give her a good scare, man."

"Lorenzo, seriously—fuck off. We'll be fine," I reply.

"We've got a few guys stationed outside the door just in case you even think of trying something," he says.

He takes a bottle of water out of his bag of snacks and screws the cap off. He waves it right in front of Ivy's eyes.

"You don't have to be so cruel to her," I hiss.

"Yes, I do," he says.

"Mmaggaahhh! Maaaagauuhh!" Ivy shouts as Lorenzo pours the water out all over her head.

My hand goes straight to my gun again, and my finger rests on the trigger. I grit my teeth as I try to fight the urge to kill him.

Ivy shivers, and there's nothing I can do. My heart hurts worse than it ever has in my life. I swore to her that I'd protect her, and already I've failed. It's the kind of failure that rips your soul apart, so I guess it's a good thing my soul doesn't exist.

Lorenzo and Terrence take their bag and leave again. Once more laughing at Ivy's expense. Once the door slams shut, I leap up, and rush to her. My thick fingers fumble as I unhook the ball gag and pull it from her mouth. My hands are shaking now. I've seen so many horrible things, but for some reason this is the worst. Watching Ivy suffer makes me want to die. But I won't kill myself in here, because then she'd be left with nothing. I'm no good for her, but I'm all she's got right now.

"You bastard!" she screams.

"Quiet, sweetheart. You want those guys to rush back in here and shove that thing in your mouth again?"

She looks down, and I watch the water droplets sliding down her red strands of hair.

I move in close and position my head just a few inches from hers. Kissing her would be the smart thing to do right now. This girl is my world tonight, and I want her to be my world forever. I raise my trembling hands and hold the sides of her face.

She whimpers. "Please...please..." she says.

"Ivy, you've got to try to stay calm, ok?"

"Why are you shaking so much?" she asks.

She shivers, and it's like I can feel that shiver running down my own spine and spreading into every part of my body.

"Because despite what you might think, watching you suffer wasn't in my game plan for tonight."

"I believe you," she whispers.

"So, you'll be quiet, right?" I ask.

"Yeah, yeah, I promise. I'll be quieter."

"Good," I whisper.

I plant a soft kiss on her forehead. But damn, do I ever want to do more than that.

"Tell me why you're helping these guys. Don't just give me some lame excuse, or a half story, or whatever. I really want to know why you took me tonight for them."

"My younger sister—she—I—"

I never talk about this with anyone. It stays bottled up inside me, where I let it fester, until I have to burst out in a display of anger and hit something or someone. But now Ivy wants me to talk about it, and I don't think I can hold it in much longer.

"Your sister?" she asks.

"Yeah, I'd rather not talk about it," I reply. It takes every ounce of willpower I've got to keep this inside me now, and not just spill my guts to Ivy. She deserves to know why I did this to her, and a good man would tell her—the whole damn sad story. But I'm not a good man. I'm a monster.

I stand up and go back to my chair. All of a sudden, I find I can't look at her. My failures with Ivy just keep mounting. She does something to me—makes my brain go all foggy in a way it ain't never done before. She clouds my judgement and makes me think impossible thoughts about what might be able to be between us. If I open up to her about my reasons for being here tonight—for doing this to her—then there's no telling what might happen next.

It's starting to feel like I might need to protect Ivy from myself.

"You can tell me when you're ready," she says. "But I expect you to do it at some point tonight. Just so you know."

"We'll see," I mumble.

She gives me a confused look, and I just shrug my shoulders. I don't want to think about what might be happening to her. I don't want to imagine that she could ever fall in love with me.

At some point tonight, I may be forced to make Ivy think I want to hurt her. Lorenzo and Terrence may demand to see proof of my loyalty to Griffon. If I keep thinking about how bad I want to make this beautiful girl mine, I won't be able to do it when I need to.

The door opens, and we both turn our heads to look at it. A man walks in, followed by two other men. They all wear black suits, with white shirts and dark ties. Their shoes are polished to a shine. The first one is tall and looks to be around my age. He's got a scar across his chin, and he's wearing a pair of glasses. His hair is short, and grey. He's the only one who seems to be armed.

He walks over to Ivy and looks her over. I try to remember if I've ever seen him before but can't place him if I have. Griffon has a lot of men at his disposal, a lot of thugs. But these guys look like the high-level thugs.

"We need you to speak to your father and show him how desperate you are for him to pay your ransom," the tall man says.

"He—He doesn't—He never talks to me. Only on my birthday," Ivy stutters.

He turns to me now. "You must be Raptor." He comes over to me and holds out his hand.

I take it, gripping it as tight as I can, which causes him to wince in pain. I'd twist his arm right out of his socket now if I could do so without getting Ivy killed.

"You've got a strong grip. Griffon is always talking about you—going off about how much he loved watching you shoot Tommy Two Face. Said you killed the guy and then just kept shooting because it seemed to give you a great deal of pleasure. Is that a true story?"

"The boss wouldn't lie to you, mister," I reply.

He clicks his tongue against his teeth several times before grinning.

"You've got a great future in the organization, Raptor. I look forward to seeing everything you do. Now please hold a gun to this girl's head while I call her daddy."

"Raptor...." Ivy says. "Please don't do—"

But it's too late. I'm out of my chair and back behind hers, holding the gun to the side of my sweet baby's head. This is just one of the many moments I may be called upon to hurt her in some way, but it's for her own good that I go through with it. Maybe she'll understand someday why I did it. Even if I'm not around to explain myself.

Ivy sobs as the tall man dials a number and holds the phone up to Ivy's face.

"Say hi to daddy," the tall man says.

"Ivy? Oh Jesus. They've really got you," a man I assume is Ivy's father says.

"Please tell my dad to come to the phone, Max," Ivy says.

I was wrong. It ain't her father. He's too busy to answer his own damn phone calls.

"Ivy, you know your father loves you, but it's gonna take some time to work this out. Ok? These men are asking for an awful lot," Max says.

"Please, please tell him to do something!" Ivy screams. I pull the gun away from her head, but the tall man sees me do it.

"Raptor, put that gun right back where it belongs," he growls.

My whole body is burning with rage as I lift the gun back to her head. I want to shoot these men, but I'm helpless—totally useless to Ivy in this situation.

"We'll figure this out, Ivy," Max says. "In the meantime, just do what you're told."

He hangs up, and leaves Ivy sitting there sobbing.

The tall man shoves the phone back in his pocket and grins.

"Daddy couldn't even be bothered to take your phone call," he says.

"He—he doesn't—he doesn't care about me," Ivy replies.

"We'll see about that."

He and his men leave the room, and I set my gun on the ground. I come around to the front and kneel before Ivy.

"You're a liar," she says.

"I know you think that, and there's nothing I can do about it right now. I'm sorry for what just happened though. I need you to believe me so we can get through this."

"Ok, I'll—I'll pretend like you mean it," she whispers hoarsely.

And then I can just no longer hold myself back. I press my lips to hers and find that she opens up to accept my tongue with no resistance at all. Maybe she's been weakened too much by the events of the night to resist, but I'd like to think she feels this thing between us just as much as I do. Our kiss is slow, and passionate, but building to something more—like a small fire that grows into a big one.

"What was that?" She asks. "Should we really have done that?"

"Yeah. Yeah, we should have," I reply.

Ivy

He held a gun to my head. Of all the things that would disqualify a potential boyfriend, that should be near the top of the list.

He held that gun to my head, and then once those guys were gone—he kissed me like he meant it. Like he wanted to spend the rest of his life kissing me. And I can't say that I don't feel the same way.

It's hard to remember why I ever thought that I didn't want to kiss him. Raptor seems to care about me deeply and is willing to do whatever it takes to get me through this night alive. Even if I don't exactly understand everything he does as it happens.

But I should just ask him to clarify some things for me...

"Why did you listen to that man when he told you to hold that gun to my head?" I ask.

"If I hadn't done it, he would have had his men kill me. And then there would be no one here to make sure you survive the night. Or however long we're trapped in this miserable place."

I close my eyes, as if I'm hoping that when I reopen them, this place will be gone, and I'll be somewhere else with Raptor. Hopefully getting to know him in some way far better than this.

"Do whatever you have to do to keep us both alive," I say.

He scoots his chair closer, curses under his breath, and then moves it right in front of mine. I suppose the cursing was because he couldn't decide how close to me that he wanted to be. My eyes wander down to his crotch, and I just can't help but notice the curve of his cock against his jeans. I suppose this is the part of my captivity where I start to think about what it would mean to die a virgin. If I wasn't chained to this chair and could move my hands, I might ask Raptor to help me out with that part. But I'm pretty sure he doesn't have the key to my chains.

Still—the wetness between my legs grows, and my body actually warms up even though I've been sitting here shivering since that man dumped water over me. And I catch myself biting my bottom lip and running my tongue over it as I stare at Raptor's mouth hoping for another kiss.

"You're really cold," he says.

"I'm not," I lie.

"You're shivering," he says.

He pulls his shirt off and tosses it to the side. His chest is covered in tattoos and scars, and I can't help but wonder what kind of monster would hurt someone so badly. I can't imagine doing that to anyone. I've never even been tempted to hurt anyone before.

He wraps the shirt around my back, and then moves his chair side by side with mine. His arm reaches across my back, and he lays his hand on my shoulder, drawing me close to him. His warmth is incredible, and I can't help but lean into him. I'm still shivering, but I feel like I'm starting to warm up.

"How do you do it?" I ask. "How do you stay so calm? You're a total badass, and I'm terrified."

"I just focus on what I have to do," he replies. "There's no time to be afraid. Not when you're in danger."

"If you care about me so much, then why can't you tell me why you brought me to these men tonight?"

He sighs heavily. "Bringing you here is going to go down as the worst mistake of my life. But when my little sister was dying of cancer and the insurance companies wouldn't pay for the experimental treatment that I thought might save her, a friend of mine introduced me to a man named Griffon. He said Griffon would give me work that would help me raise a lot of cash fast. I didn't question it at all. I just took every damn job Griffon offered me, no matter how many times it involved killing one of his enemies."

"You've killed people," I say. Maybe I should be suspicious of this man, and I shouldn't be leaning on him. But his warmth, manly scent, and gentle touch when it comes to me just keeps drawing me back in closer to him.

"Yes, I have. And I will do it again if I need to," he says.

His words make me shudder. "Oh," I whisper.

"I was desperate to keep my sister alive, even though the chances of it weren't that great. But I couldn't just not try. But I know I'm not some damn hero, Ivy, and whatever happens tonight, I don't want you to think I am. Ok?"

I don't want to answer him. He might have brought me here, but he's doing everything he can to keep me alive. So, by the end of the night, Raptor might be my hero, and there won't be a damn thing either he or I can do about it.

"You know the weirdest thing right now? I'm starting to worry that I'm gonna die a virgin. That's silly, right?" As I say it, I feel that warm tingling sensation between my legs. I rest my head on his bare chest, and sigh. Maybe this is what is meant by Stockholm syndrome. Maybe that's why I want to be so close to him right now.

But I'm pretty sure it's not. My reasons for feeling this way are because of him, and the way he treats me.

Raptor runs a finger up and down my arm, slow and soft. By what feels like instinct, I open my legs slightly and take in a deep breath. I know where I'd rather his finger be, and it's not my arm.

The musty scent of the warehouse seems to go away, and all I can smell is him—that musky, manly scent.

Raptor's finger moves from my arm to my lips, and I catch myself moaning as he traces them softly. This is so unimaginably wrong. Later tonight, those other men are going to come back in here and take advantage of me. I'm sure of it. Yet here I am just about to allow Raptor to have his way with me. I know he wants it just as bad as I do. His touch leaves me trembling and aching to be filled.

"Please," I whisper.

He leans down and kisses me gently, and I moan into his mouth. He brushes his lips against mine, and then presses his tongue inside my mouth. I can taste the saltiness of my own tears, and the faint hint of blood from where I chewed on my bottom lip a bit too hard.

His hand wraps gently around my throat as he kisses me. I feel him moving his body closer to mine as he lets go of my throat and moves onto my breast. He pinches my nipple, and I gasp as unknown sensations shoot through me. I feel like I'm being torn in two. I want to run my hands through his hair and pull him close to me. But I'm chained to this chair, and I can't move.

"Ivy," he whispers. "What do you want me to do?" He rests his upper lip on my bottom one. His breath warms my skin.

I want to cry out and beg for him to take me. But I don't know how that would even work right now unless he somehow frees me from this damn chair.

"I—I want—I want your fingers on my—"

I don't even have to say the rest. His hand glides across the fabric of my dress until he reaches the bottom. Then he moves to my leg and slides up the dress...

Is this really happening right now?

I feel his fingers running up and down my thigh, and I'm shaking so badly that I can barely hold myself together. I bite my lip, and grit my teeth, trying to focus on something else. But it's pointless to try and chase these feelings away.

"Your skin is so damn soft," he growls. "I almost feel like I'm gonna break you somehow just by touching you."

"I want to be broken," I whisper.

Our foreheads press together now, and his hand moves to between my legs and slides through the side of my thin panties. He presses the pad of his thumb to my clit, and I gasp. He slowly rubs over it, and I start to shake uncontrollably."

"Tell me how that feels," he says.

I close my eyes and let out a long sigh. I can't stop thinking about what he's doing to me. It's making me crazy, and I want more. I want to tell him that, but I'm not sure if I can. Nothing has felt both more wrong and more right in my entire life, and it's gonna drive me crazy.

"It's incredible," I moan.

He stops rubbing my clit, and I can feel the wetness of my juices soaking my panties. I open my eyes and see Raptor staring at me. He looks like he's in pain, and I know he is. He knows what he's doing to me, and he's torturing me. I've never wanted anyone to look at me like that before.

"What do you want?" he asks.

"More," I say. "I want you to keep going."

"Are you sure?" he asks.

"Yes. Please..."

He slides several of his thick fingers inside me, and the lower half of my body thrusts forward instantly. He holds my chair down so I don't go flying, and I rest my head on his chest as he rubs the inside of my tunnel. My own fingers have been inside of me before, so it's not like this is the first time I've felt something inside me. But it feels like the first. It's the first time a man has been inside me, and the combination of the sensations and the knowledge that it's happening makes me cry out in ecstasy. My skin is so damn sensitive, and for the first time in my life it seems I'm able to know what true pleasure is.

"Oh, God!" I moan. "Please! Don't stop!"

"You're so tight," he groans.

He pushes his fingers inside me faster, and I'm amazed at how much more intense the feeling becomes. His thumb goes back to my clit, and I whimper as he begins to rub me harder.

"Fuck," he growls. "I'm gonna cum."

I lift my head off his chest and stare at him. He stares back, and I feel like I'm seeing him for the first time. His eyes are wide, and there's a look of pure lust on his face.

"You're gonna cum just from touching me?" I whisper.

He breathes hard and fast. "Yeah, yeah, baby girl. I am."

Knowing that I did this to a man sends me right over the edge, and I cum so hard that I can't even scream. I just buck and squirm in my chair, my whole body shaking and quivering.

I look down and catch Raptor opening his jeans. His cock is huge, and it springs out and points straight up. He slams his hand over the top and I watch as cum oozes through the spaces between his fingers.

Once we're done, we both take deep breaths, and sigh.

"I didn't know a guy could do that," I say.

"It's rare, but it does happen. I hope you won't hold it against me."

I find myself giggling softly at that one. "Hold it against you? The fact that I turned you on so much you came without even touching yourself? There's no way I could hold that against you. But you better find something to wipe your hands off on."

He takes his shirt off my back, and I laugh as he gets ready to wipe his hand off with it. "No, no. Use my dress," I say. "Maybe it'll give you some street cred with those other guys if they realize you left a cum stain on me."

"You are a naughty girl, Ivy Walker," he says as he indulges my request and playfully wipes his hand on the lower half of the front of my dress, leaving a nice creamy looking wet spot on me. He doesn't bother rubbing it in all the way, so it definitely looks obvious what it is. "I haven't been with a woman in years, and I haven't touched myself in longer than that. I guess that was the release my body has been dying for, and you gave it to me."

"Wow," I say. "I'm good."

"Damn right you are." He kisses the top of my head.

And my crazy mind gets to work on thinking that maybe this is all somehow fate making things happen in a really messed up way. Maybe I'm just losing my mind and holding on to whatever hope about Raptor I can conjure in my mind is helping me survive. That alone makes it worth it, but maybe it's worth a lot more...

Raptor

Lorenzo and Terrence return, but I just sit there beside Ivy with her head on my chest. I don't care if they see us like this. This won't be the thing that makes them kill us anyway. As Ivy said, they'll probably cheer for me at this sight.

Terrence stands before us, throws his head back, and laughs. "Ahhh, man, don't you two make a cute couple? What the hell are you doing in here, Raptor? You get this girl to suck your dick yet?"

Neither Ivy nor I say a single word. I just keep my lips sealed tight and do my best to show no emotion at all. But it's getting harder and harder to contain the murderous rage that's building inside me. I'm so fucking tired of these assholes. They've had their fun. This shit has gone on long enough.

Terrence looks down at the splotch of white cream on the bottom of Ivy's dress that has yet to dry up.

"Good job, Raptor. You got her mouth ready for us, huh?"

Terrence unzips his pants and whips out his cock. But before he can try to force it down Ivy's throat, I've already jumped up and knocked him to the ground. Now I'm just beating his face in and he's crying and begging me to stop.

I hear Ivy gasp and then cry out as I slam my fist into Terrence's face. He goes limp and stops moving. I reach down and grab his cock, which is still hard, and give it a twist till he's conscious again and screaming.

Lorenzo has just been standing nearby chuckling to himself the whole time. But soon I feel a gun on the back of my head.

"Let go of his dick, asshole," Lorenzo growls. "I gotta admit it was pretty funny to watch, but Terrence here is my partner and I gotta take care of him."

I let go of Terrence's cock, and spit in his face. "Stay away from the girl. She's not yours."

"She's not yours either, Raptor. Come on. Get back up and do your duty of guarding the girl. That's all you're supposed to be doing in here. I ought to shoot you both for taking part in extracurricular activities I didn't give permission for."

I stand up slowly and glare at Lorenzo. "You want to fight me? Let's do it. You've been a pain in my ass since day one. I'm sick of you. And I'm sick of you telling me what to do."

His gun is aimed at my chest now, and he steps forward and presses it against my heart.

"I don't want to have to do this to you, buddy," he says. "You're too valuable to Griffon, and I'm sure he wouldn't be happy if I killed his number one hitman."

I wish he wouldn't say such things in front of Ivy. I don't want her to constantly be reminded of my darkness—not when I'm trying to conjure up some kind of light to show her instead.

I grab Lorenzo by the throat and squeeze. Some force in the universe must be watching out for me, because he doesn't shoot me.

"Ok, ok. When all this is over, buddy, we'll have our fight. And we'll do it with our bare hands," Lorenzo says.

"I'll snap your damn head right off your body," I growl as I let go of his throat and sit back down next to Ivy.

Lorenzo kicks Terrence. "Get up, jackass."

Terrence groans, and tries to rise to his feet, but falls right back down while reaching out and grabbing hold of Lorenzo's pants.

"How much longer is all this gonna take?" I ask. "Why the hell is it taking so long for the mayor to send the damn ransom money and agree to taking Griffon on as an advisor?"

"So that's what—" Ivy starts to say before stopping herself. I'm sure she's thinking about the nightmare this city will descend into if a guy like Griffon pulls the strings of her soon to be puppet father.

"It turns out, the mayor isn't all that concerned about the girl. He's much more worried about being forced to take advice from Griffon," Lorenzo says. "I bet we could kill the girl and he'd never even think about her again."

Ivy sobs. I take her hand and squeeze it, doing my best to comfort her in some small way while these guys are still in the room. Once they leave, I'll put my arm around her again and pull her in close. Because despite our current situation, my cock is hard again, and I'm already back to thinking about what it would be like to slide my manhood inside of her. Those warm juices, and perfect amount of pressure and friction for my cock would make me explode in an instant.

"You'd better get back upstairs and help Griffon deal with the mayor," I say.

"He put us in charge of her, and you're just working for us right now. So, don't tell us what to do," Lorenzo says. "We're your boss right now, Raptor. Not the other way around."

"I really have to use the restroom," Ivy says. "Can I please do that?"

"Pee all over your chair for all I care, girl," Lorenzo says.

"Unlock her chains and give me the key. I'll take her to the restroom, and then chain her back up. I promise," I reply. "That way you can go take care of Terrence and do whatever else the hell you want."

Lorenzo stands before Ivy and runs his fingers through her hair. She whimpers, and I watch as he twirls a strand of her hair around his index finger. Damn, I need to kill this guy. Somehow, someday—I'm gonna kill him.

"She sure is pretty," he says. "I can see why you wanted to shove your cock into her pretty little mouth."

He releases her and digs in his pocket for something. When he pulls the key out, he tosses it on the ground at my feet.

"Take her to the restroom, but come right back here, and chain her up again. We might have to do another video call with daddy soon, even though he doesn't seem to give a damn about her. Maybe if he sees a knife to her throat, he'll change his mind."

Lorenzo yanks Terrence up, and once they're out of the room, I release Ivy from her chains.

She tries to stand up but falls back down. She reaches out and grabs my leg.

"Please help me," she pleads. "My legs have fallen asleep."

"Ok, sweetheart," I reply as I take her hands, and pull her up. She immediately wraps her arms around me. I feel my damn thing straining against my pants again as her soft breasts push against my flesh. The things I would do to them if the circumstances were different. They're not the largest breasts in the world, but they look perfect for sliding my dick between and then cumming all over her soft, pale skin.

But I need to focus on getting her to the restroom, so I pick her up and sling her over my shoulder. She shrieks in surprise as I do it but doesn't struggle.

"I gotta carry you like this to put on a show for the guards," I say.

"Yeah, sure," she replies. "It's all for the guards."

I carry her out past the guards, and they don't say a word.

The whole time we walk down the hallway, she keeps clinging to me and sighing softly. I can't wait to get her naked and fucked, but I know that's not going to happen right now. If I could, I'd rip her dress off her small body, and take her against the wall of the bathroom stall. In a better world, she could scream all she wants, and I could watch those green eyes of hers roll around in her skull while I make her mine over and over again.

Yeah, that would be a more perfect world. But sadly, it's not the one we're living in.

Ivy

Raptor carries me into the restroom and sets me down. He locks the door behind us.

"Go ahead," he says. "I'll just be waiting here for you."

"Oh, you don't want to come into the stall with me, huh?" I tease.

"I think I'd rather wait outside the door," he answers. "I won't be able to control myself if I go in there with you."

I open the stall door, and turn back towards him, managing a teasing wink. Despite the night I've had, Raptor has been the one thing keeping me alive—keeping me interested in still being alive.

I step into the stall and shut the door. I take care of my business, and then sit there on the toilet for a while just silently praying to get out of this place and if it's at all possible—to be with Raptor. It's crazy how much I want to be his girl.

"You ok in there?" He asks.

"Yeah, just thinking," I reply. "If my dad doesn't pay the ransom, these guys will just kill me, right?"

"I don't want you thinking about that anymore, sweetheart," he replies. "Just focus on staying as calm as possible and not giving them an excuse to try and hurt you. You saw what I did to Terrence, so you know I can take care of you."

"Yeah, I know," I whisper.

I swing the stall door open, and gesture for Raptor to come in. He steps towards me with a grin on his face the size of the moon. I slide my hand up his arm, and he pulls me up and close to him.

"What should we do in here, baby girl?" He growls. "I'm having an awful hard time right now. I'm trying to stay calm, but I can't do it around you."

He pulls my hand up to his bare chest and rests my palm over his heart. His cock is already pushing up against his pants, and I can feel the warmth of it through his jeans.

"I've never been with a man before," I whisper. "And I really don't want to die without having a chance to feel you inside of me." I kick my panties off the rest of the way.

He leads me out of the stall and lifts me onto one of the sinks. Our eyes lock, and he takes my face in his hands. I feel his pulse through his palms, and it seems to move into me. If I was in a doctor's office, they might think I was having a panic attack or something, because I'm breathing so fast and shallow. My chest is heaving as I wait to see what Raptor will do to me.

"Baby girl, you're not gonna die," he whispers. "I promise. Just trust me."

I nod and reach out to touch his lips.

"Please, kiss me," I say. "Make me yours."

His eyes are full of lust and hunger as he leans down and presses his mouth against mine. I feel his tongue push its way between my lips, and I moan in response. I run my hands down his back and hold on to him tightly. I want to memorize every inch of him, so I can remember the feeling of his lips against mine, and the feel of his warm body pressed against me.

Someone is talking outside the door, but I can't make out what they're saying. Their voices pass quickly though.

Raptor groans as he kisses me. It's a primal groan that makes it sound like his body is begging for release. Will he allow himself to have me? I'm ready to give myself to him if only he'll take the chance...

He breaks from our kiss and kneels before the sink as he gently pulls me to the edge of it. I lean back on the mirror and hold my breath as I wait for his next move. His mouth is on my sex in an instant, and his tongue lashes across my slit.

"Oh fuck," I moan.

I can't believe how good his mouth feels on me. I grab his head and pull him closer, wanting him to devour me. I want him to make me his.

"Raptor, please," I beg. "I need you."

"I need you too, Ivy," he replies. "You're so beautiful. So, fucking hot. I can't help myself. I love your pussy. I love how soft and tight it is. I love how wet you get when I lick you."

"There will be plenty of time to lick me later," I reply. "I want you inside of me."

"I love that you're not afraid to ask for what you want," he replies.

"It wouldn't be like that with anyone else," I reply. "I thought I'd never want this with anyone, but now I'm—I'm just—-"

"Overwhelmed," he replies. "I know because I am too."

He goes back to rolling his tongue on my slit, and my body jerks forward. I grab the sides of the sink, and squeeze my eyes shut.

"Don't stop," I whimper. "Please don't stop."

"I won't," he says. "I want to feel you cum all over my face."

"Oh god, yes," I moan. "Yes, oh god, Raptor, I'm gonna—-"

"Cum for me, Ivy," he orders. "Come for me."

"Ohhhhhhh!" I scream as my orgasm hits me. My legs tremble and shake, and my body quivers uncontrollably. Raptor's tongue keeps moving, and I grab his hair and pull his face even tighter against my sex.

"Oh my god," I moan. "I'm cumming again."

"I know," he groans. "I can taste you. And baby girl, you taste like heaven."

He pulls his face away and stands up. I open my eyes and watch him undo his pants. His cock springs free, and it looks like it's about to burst. He reaches down and grabs my hand. He helps me down off the sink and leads me back into a stall. We're lucky no one has come looking for us yet. I guess even all these tough guys are afraid to come into a woman's restroom and harass her while she's doing things that men often think women don't do. And that's our advantage, because this restroom is the only place in this building that Raptor and I can be together where it's safe.

Raptor locks us in the stall and looks down at me. My back is pressed up against the wall, and my body is buzzing.

"What do you want, baby?" He asks. "We don't have to do a damn thing you don't want. But I'll tell you that the best thing for me right now is to be inside you."

I jolt, as if I've been struck by lightning or something. Maybe it's all the electrical energy built up inside of me now.

"But I want to do more than just fuck you," he continues. "I want to make you mine. I want to make you feel loved and safe, even if tonight is our only time together."

"Oh god," I whisper. "I want you too—I want to be yours."

"Then let me take care of you," he says. "Let me show you how much I want you."

He lifts me up. My legs go instinctively around his waist, and I can feel his manhood pressing up against my skin—hot and filled with lust—lust that seems reserved for me.

"Put your arms around my neck," he orders.

I wrap my hands around his neck and pull myself tightly against him. He runs his hands over my ass, and I gasp as he positions his cock against my entrance. He kisses me as he enters my sex, and I feel my insides stretch to accommodate his girth. It's like he's made of steel, and I'm nothing but a feather. I can't believe how good he feels inside of me.

"Oh," I moan. "I can't take any more of you." It feels like heaven all right, but it's also painful the more he pushes into me.

"Just relax, baby. Just let me love you," he growls.

He begins to move inside of me, and I start to feel like separation at this point would only drive me mad. He holds me tight, and his hips pound against me, driving me towards my release. My fingers dig into the skin of his back, but it doesn't affect him at all even though I can feel the blood beneath my fingertips.

"Raptor, please," I cry out. "Please, don't stop."

He pounds into me, and I moan loudly as my orgasm hits me. Raptor moans with me, and his thrusts grow harder and faster. He slams himself deep inside of me, and I'm overwhelmed by the feeling of being full. I've never felt so full in my life. I can feel his heartbeat against my skin, and his cock pulsing inside my pussy.

It's like I've been waiting all my life for this one man—this man who knows how to take me and guide me in every new sensation rippling through me right now. I'm drowning in pleasure, and it's too much. I'm going to lose control.

We pant together as he thrusts. Then his mouth is back on mine, and he's kissing me deeply as his body trembles. He doesn't slow down. He just keeps fucking me. I try to keep my eyes open, but it's too hard. My vision blurs, and I can barely hear what Raptor is saying.

"Ivy, I'm gonna cum," he groans. "Are you ready? Are you ready for me to fill you with my seed?"

"Yes!" I cry. "Yes, I'm ready! Fill me with your cum, Raptor! Give it to me!"

"That's it, baby girl," he groans.

He erupts inside me, and I feel it filling me up as his cock continues to pulse. His body jerks, and his lips part from mine. He lets out a low moan, and I feel him push deeper. He fills me completely, and I feel the pressure building up inside of me. My pussy clenches around his cock, and I feel the need to cum rising up inside of me.

Even though he's already finished, he stays with me, and lets me ride the wave of yet another orgasm. He presses his mouth to my ear: "I love you, Ivy," he whispers. "Can't help it."

He holds me there and we both tremble against each other. When we go back out to return to the room I'm being held in, the danger will feel real once more. Tonight, could be the night I die, but at least I'll know that I was his even if only for a short while.

One thing I know for sure – my panties are staying on the floor of this restroom.

*

We head back towards the room I'm being held in. Outside the door, the two men—Terrence and Lorenzo—are standing over the bodies of the guards.

"What happened?" Raptor asks.

"Oh, you're back after all. Maybe I didn't have to kill these two assholes then," Lorenzo says as calmly as if he hasn't just killed two men.

"I took her to the restroom, just like you said I could," Raptor replies. "There was no need for this. You can trust me, Lorenzo. I've got no choice but to be loyal to Griffon."

I know he's not loyal to Griffon at all, or at least I don't think he is. My stomach flutters as I consider the possibility that Raptor actually means to be here, and just decided he wanted to use me. But then I take a deep breath and remember the sound of his voice when he told me he loved me. He meant it—there was no way it was a lie. I hadn't said it back, because in the moment, I was too scared to consider it and I still am. Even if he means it.

Lorenzo claps Raptor on the back. "That was an awful long restroom break. These two idiots should have gone to check on you, and they didn't. Their deaths are on you, buddy. I hope the little slut's pussy was worth it."

"Fuck you," Raptor growls. "Just let me get her back in the room and into the chair."

"Of course," Lorenzo says. He steps out of the way and we go back into the room.

Raptor leads me back to my chair. "I've gotta chain you back up, Ivy," he says. "I'm sorry."

"Don't worry about it," I say. "I'll be okay."

Lorenzo and Terrence clap. "Such a tender scene," Lorenzo hisses. "I'll remember it for the rest of my life. Just chain her back up and get back to watching the little whore."

I clench my hands into fists and dig my nails into my palms. If I could, I'd kill Lorenzo and Terrence. It would probably feel amazing to choke the life out of them, or shoot them, or...

No. I'm not sure I could do it. Even as much as I hate them. I would only want to severely hurt them, but not kill. I'll leave that part up to Raptor.

Raptor chains me up as I was before – chain around my legs, and a chain wrapped around me and the back of the chair.

"She looks so sexy," Lorenzo whispers. "You did good, Raptor."

"Shut up," Raptor snaps.

Lorenzo smiles. "And I'm glad you're taking care of her. We'll send her back to her daddy pregnant with somebody's baby. Before we return her, I'm thinking everyone in this building gets a turn. That's what Griffon told me is gonna happen to her anyway, whether you like it or not."

I know that every time they say this, Raptor's body stiffens, and I can see him straining to hold his anger in—clenched fists, clenched teeth, and I swear he's turning red. But rather than beat Lorenzo up like he did with Terrence, he keeps it all in—probably because the mention of this Griffon guy.

Several men burst into the room with guns.

"Alright, boss' orders. The girl is being brought upstairs. Her daddy's sending someone to negotiate her release."

The tension drains out of me. Finally, my father is sending someone to get me out of this place. But of course, he's not coming himself. What would happen if a reporter followed him? Or

Griffon recorded the proceedings and used them to blackmail him again? No, my father doesn't care enough about me to come himself. Still, this is good news.

"Raptor, you carry the girl upstairs," Lorenzo says. "Chair and all."

Raptor leans in close to me and whispers in my ear. "It's gonna be okay now. I promise you."

He sounds like he believes it, and that's enough for me. This man—this powerful, confident, sexy man told me he loves me. And I believe him.

Raptor picks up my chair with me in it and I go for a ride out of the room and down the hall. He carries me so effortlessly, even up the stairs. The other men follow behind us, and I'm aware that at any moment one of them could get a little trigger happy and put an end to me, and probably Raptor too. The way he's treated me tonight has put him at risk, and I feel responsible for it.

The heat between my legs returns, and I can't wait to get out of here and let him take me over and over again. He can do it all night—I know I can handle it.

Raptor

I get Ivy up the stairs, and the guards outside Griffon's office hold the door open for us. His office is nothing crazy—just a desk and a couple chairs. And a cabinet full of guns and a safe full of money.

"Set her down across from me, Raptor," Griffon says in his typical low voice. He coughs on his cigar smoke, and as I set Ivy down, he blows it directly at her and she starts coughing too. This and so many other things are definitely grounds to kill him. He's playing with my girl's life tonight, and once I get Ivy out of here; I will hunt Griffon and every one of his men down. Then I'll go home to Ivy and make her scream in ecstasy. She deserves pleasure, and only I should give it to her.

Ain't nobody else in this world qualified.

Griffon clears his throat and laughs. "You're going to be my guest for a while, you little bitch," he says to Ivy.

I stand there behind her, keeping my hands on her smooth, bare shoulders.

"Has Raptor been taking good care of you, Miss Walker?" Griffon asks, suddenly switching to a more polite tone. Though even his polite tone sounds like a snake. He looks like a snake too—tall and thin and pale.

"Yes, sir," Ivy says.

"Good. That's good," Griffon hisses. "He's my best man—loyal to a fault too, I tell ya. He'll do anything for me. Ain't that right, Raptor?"

I curse silently to myself, before replying with, "Yes, sir."

I'm sure he's trying to make Ivy hate me now, by making me seem like a loyal soldier who will get down and suck his damn dick at a moment's notice if that's what he wanted.

But I won't do it. I love Ivy, and I want to protect her. I'm already doing it, and I'll keep protecting her until I die.

"Ivy, honey, I know you've had a rough time of it. But don't worry, I'm going to fix all of that," Griffon says. "I'm gonna make your daddy pay for what he's done to you."

My stomach is fluttering, and breathing is getting shallow. This isn't like me. I'm normally calm in all situations, but this—this feeling inside me now must be love. It must be love, because I'm terrified for Ivy. I've already told her that I love her, and though she didn't say it back, I know that over time she'll feel the same way. But only if I get her out of this night alive.

The door swings open, and I whirl around to see who's coming in. A small man in a suit that I recognize as the mayor's assistant Ivy was made to talk to earlier is shoved into the room. He shrieks as he falls to the floor and scrambles back up only to fall right back down. The thug behind him shoves a gun into his back.

"Our dear mayor couldn't even come himself to save his daughter," Griffon says. "I'm quite disappointed to see that he's sent scum like you to handle negotiations."

"I—I—there are—-there are—-ahhh—police waiting outside. They're ready to come in at a moment's notice. I was just sent in to see if you could be reasonable and let the girl go in exchange for a larger sum of cash then what you even asked for," the small man says. "We can then put all this talk of you being an advisor to the mayor to rest."

This is good. Ivy's father is willing to put up a lot of money to save her. But I know money isn't what Griffon wants. He clears his throat and walks over to the little man. He kneels beside him.

"You and your boss know what I want. If I don't get that then the girl dies, and I'll leak the story of the mayor's unwanted secret daughter to the press. How would he like that?"

Ivy shudders beneath my hands.

"It's okay, sweetie," I say. It's all I think I can get away with saying right now—just a little something to calm her down and reassure her that I'm still here, and I'll fight for her till my last moment on Earth.

"We can't appoint you to an advisory role to the mayor. It's just not possible. Think of the scandal that alone would bring!" the little man says.

"Max, isn't it?" Griffon asks.

Max nods.

"Make it happen, buddy. I don't have to be a known advisor. We can do everything in secret, since that's how your boss prefers to work anyway. This girl is proof of that."

"But..." Max says.

"What's the matter, buddy? Can't get it up for your boss' daughter?" Griffon asks. "I bet you've been dying to fuck her for a long time. If you convince your boss to accept my terms, I'll be happy to let you have that little pussy for thirty seconds, since that's all you'll last anyway."

Griffon laughs as Max whimpers.

"There's—there's no deal," Max says.

Griffon kicks Max in the stomach. "What do you mean, no deal? You wanna watch the girl die before I shoot you? If that's what you want, I'll be more than happy to do it, you little worm!"

"No!" Max shouts.

But he's too late. Griffon goes back to his desk, pulls a gun from the drawer, and aims it at Ivy. My heart stops. Can I be faster than him? Is he really gonna do it?

I can't take the chance that he actually does it. And even though I know I'm about to die for what I'm gonna do, I've got no choice but to do it.

I whip my gun out of the holster faster than I ever have in my life and shoot Griffon in the chest. He has a startled look on his face as he falls backward.

The next thing I know, a bullet hits me in the back. It tears through me and causes me to collapse to the ground as Ivy screams "No!"

Everything...my love...will never...be lost...

Ivy

There's gunfire outside the room. The police must have decided to storm Griffon's building. Lucky for me, Griffon's armed thugs leave the office to shoot at the cops. I rock backwards until I fall to the ground.

"Somebody, please help me!" I scream. "I'm in here!"

Max crawls over to me. "Just shut the hell up, girl! You'll get us killed!"

"Fuck you," I reply. I spit in Max's face.

But I don't really care about Max right now. I need someone in here who can help Griffon. So, I just keep on screaming at the top of my lungs.

Max shoves me towards Raptor. Which makes at least one thing Max has done right.

My stomach feels like it's on fire right now, and tears are just pouring out of me. But I have to speak. I have to tell Raptor that I love him.

"I love you.... I love you...damn it, Raptor...I love you too...You're the only reason I'm still alive right now."

Raptor's eyelids flutter in response. He heard me, and I'm grateful for that much at least.

"Someone will be here soon to help you. You just gotta stay alive for me, okay? Let me the be the one to keep you alive now. Please, Raptor..."

"It's—-it's Joseph..." he says.

Oh my God! He's not dead!

"Hang on, Joseph. Please...please...I'm begging you."

His eyes close again, and all I can think right now is that there's so much blood all around me. His blood...

I close my eyes too. "I love you, Joseph," I say, even stronger and more confident than before.

*

I don't know how long I lay there on the floor of Griffon's office. But someone eventually comes and carries me out of the room. I see an E.M.T. working on my love, but he doesn't seem to be getting anywhere. Still, I'm hauled out of there screaming and I can't see the end result of the E.M.T.'s work.

The cop carries me outside, and someone breaks the chains on my chair, setting me free. I stand up on wobbly legs and run back towards the building screaming, but a cop drags me back. Out of the corner of my eye, I see the bodies of Lorenzo and Terrence.

"You need to go to the hospital, young lady," the cop says.

"There's a man in there...he was the man I was lying next to. I need to see him. I need to know he's alive."

"Pretty sure everyone in there works for Griffon, sweetie. You don't want nothing to do with those scumbags."

I'm dragged off and put in the back of an ambulance. The ambulance speeds off with sirens blaring, and I sob as I realize I may never see Joseph again.

*

I'm checked out at the hospital, but I turn down the more thorough examination, because I don't want them to find evidence that I had sex with Joseph. I tell the cops that nothing happened to me other than being chained up for most of the night. They do ask me about Joseph—If I saw who shot him. I tell them it was one of Griffon's guards.

"Who was the man who kidnapped you?" the officer asks as I sit on the exam table, smacking feet against the side of it.

"I never saw him," I lie. "I was blindfolded and thrown into a trunk. They didn't take the blindfold off me until we got there. Can I please see Joseph now? Please?"

"You mean Joseph Raptor Gianelli? He worked for Griffon, yes?"

"I don't know. Maybe. Can I just see him?"

"Sorry, sweetheart. He's in the operating room, and once he wakes up, we're gonna have to ask him some questions about his involvement in all this," the officer replies.

My heart sinks into my stomach, and I smack my feet harder against the exam table. Tears stream down my face. "Please don't charge him with anything. The only thing he did tonight was make sure I stayed alive."

"Do you know why you were kidnapped?"

I shake my head. "Absolutely no idea. But I know that Griffon was trying to get something out of the mayor."

The cop scribbles something down. "Yeah, that's what the mayor's assistant Max told us. He also said he never saw you in his entire life and had no idea what you were being held for. But if you're covering up for somebody, honey—well, we'll find out anyway sooner or later."

I take a deep breath. "Ok. Well, I'm sorry I can't help you anymore."

"You got anyone to take you home?"

"No. I'll just take the bus," I reply.

"Not a good idea after what you've been through. Once the nurse clears you, we'll find someone to give you a ride home."

"I'd rather stay at the hospital," I reply. "I'll just sit in the lobby and wait for Joseph to come out of surgery."

"This guy is that important to you, huh?"

I nod. "He's my hero."

*

I sit in the lobby of the E.R. for several hours. Eventually, the E.R. nurse tells me Joseph is out of surgery, but if I'm not family, I can't see him.

"I'm his fiancée," I tell the nurse. "We're getting married next week."

Of course, it's a lie, but I hope it comes true.

"Ok, you can see him then. He's sleeping right now, but you can go in there. Just follow me."

I follow the nurse into the recovery room and see Joseph lying in his hospital bed hooked up to all kinds of machines.

I slam my hand against my mouth. "Oh my God," I say.

The nurse checks his vital signs and then leaves the room. I pull a chair up to his bedside, sit down, and place my hand on top of his.

"I hope you can hear me right now. I lied to get back here. I guess we're getting married next week." I squeeze his hand as I say it. "You saved my life tonight, and there's no man on the planet I'd rather be with than the one who kept me alive. My father certainly didn't help any, so I'm here only because of you."

His eyes open, and he turns his head to look at me, but winces as he does so.

"Oh fuck," he groans. "That hurts. But it's worth it to look at you."

I stand up and assault his face with kisses.

He chuckles. "I'm not a good guy, Ivy. You probably shouldn't put your hopes on me. I'll only get you in trouble."

"The good kind of trouble," I reply.

I notice his blanket is tented, and I slide my hand underneath it and grab his cock.

"Oh, that still feels good," he says.

"I bet," I reply.

I get up and lock the door to the recovery room, then sit back down beside him.

"That will give us some time, at least, in case the nurse comes back. I might not have much time, so I'll just make this quick."

I kiss him on the lips, and then head for the end of his bed. I lift up the blanket, and his hospital gown. I see his cock sticking straight up, and I stroke it gently.

"Fuck, you're beautiful," he says.

"So are you," I reply.

"Go slow," he warns.

I lean forward and lick the head of his cock. He groans and grabs my hair. "Don't tease me like that," he growls.

I lean in again and begin sucking him off. His hands tighten around my head, and he moans loudly.

"I love how you do that," he says. "Your mouth feels so good."

I suck harder, and he groans louder. I can feel his cock growing in my mouth. I grab his balls, massaging them as I continue to suck him off.

"Ivy...oh fuck..."

I know what's coming, and I want it. So, I keep sucking.

"I'm gonna cum soon, baby," he whispers.

He bucks his hips and begins to shoot his load into my mouth. I swallow every drop, and I moan as I taste his hot seed.

When he finishes, I crawl over him, and lay my head on his chest.

"You're the only woman I can love. Just have this feeling about you," he says. "You damn near killed me just now, but it would have been a sweet death."

"You got shot in the back, and the bullet missed your heart. And you certainly did not get shot in your dick."

He coughs, and chuckles.

"Yeah, I'm right about you. And I heard you say we're getting married next week."

"Well, it was just a lie I had to tell to get back here..."

"Ivy, will you please marry me? Until I saw you, I was starting to feel like I didn't have a reason to live anymore. I was ready to throw myself in the way of a bullet. But you—-you're my girl—you're my reason—the reason I'm still breathing. Please say yes..."

"Of course, I'll marry you, as soon as they let you out of here, we can do it. I don't even care if the cops are hauling you off to jail for working for Griffon. I'll still marry you, and maybe I'll get to visit you in a private room..."

He laughs again and runs his fingers through my hair.

"I'll get out of it somehow, and then we'll get out of here. As far away from trouble as we can. We'll find some small country town we can disappear to and just make love all day."

"Sounds good to me," I whisper.

Epilogue—Raptor

One Year Later

It's been a year since I took Ivy Rose Gianelli hostage for Griffon. And just a few days away from our first anniversary as a married couple. Ivy made her father talk to the police on my behalf and keep me from getting arrested for working for Griffon. They have no idea of all the things I did for that man, and even if they did – they'd have no proof.

Just like I promised her I would, I found a small town along the East coast that we could just hide out in and start all over.

We've lived there ever since.

I'm sitting on the couch in our apartment, reading a book. It's a warm night, and I can hear Ivy snoring softly beside me with her head resting in my lap. It's the first moment of peace we've had since our twin girls Sophia and Sylvia were born.

The book is an electrician textbook, but I can't study right now. I'm too obsessed with the girl beside me. So obsessed that my thoughts are always of her and our little family. And also, of how Ivy and I can make more beautiful babies together.

My cock strains against my jeans as usual. I set my textbook down and undo my pants to create some "room to grow". My hands work their way through Ivy's hair, and she moans softly.

"Hey, you," she says quietly.

"Hi beautiful," I reply back.

She laughs. "I just gave birth to twins a month ago. So, I'm not really feeling beautiful right now."

"Well, you are beautiful, so deal with it," I growl.

"Oh, so feisty," she says. "I think I like it."

She sits up and rubs her eyes. When she's done, I kiss her, softly at first—but soon we get into our usual "ain't no way in hell we can hold back" state of intense passion. Ivy climbs into my lap and we continue our make out session. Our fingers entwine, and I feel her breasts pressed against my chest.

I break away from our kiss and look at her—just look at my gorgeous wife.

"So, damn stunning," I say. "Just the most perfect woman on the planet. Nah—in the universe."

She giggles.

"Well, right now I'd love to have that perfect cock of yours inside me," she says. Her hair covers her eyes, and I tuck it behind her ear, and she gives me the biggest grin in the world. "Do you think you can help me out?"

I don't reply with words. She sighs contentedly as I pull her t-shirt over her head, and then unhook her bra. Her breasts have swollen up because of the babies, and her nipples are rock hard.

I lick one, and she groans.

"Oh, yeah, baby. That feels so good," she says.

I suck her other nipple into my mouth, and she arches her back and grabs my hair.

"Take me, honey," she moans. "But do it quietly so the twins don't wake up."

"They're in their nursery with the door closed. And they sleep like logs."

"For now, they do," she says with a giggle.

I slide my hand down her stomach. The scent of her arousal fills the air. Pre-cum is leaking out of me like crazy, and I need to have her.

She climbs off me and makes a striptease show out of pulling off her yoga pants. I go to her and toss her over my shoulder. She makes a little squeak of surprise as I carry her to the bedroom and lay her on our bed.

"Tell me again how you could never love another woman," she says.

"You're my life, and you saved my life," I say. "From the second I saw you; I had this feeling deep down that you would. You're my girl, and I will never let you go."

She smiles. "That's what I want to hear. But it was you who saved me."

"We'll have to agree that we saved each other," I reply.

"Yes, we will," she says.

I gently slide inside her and I'm instantly swept up in the feeling of her warmth and wetness. Her pussy hugs my cock tight, and we kiss as our bodies rock against each other. I start thrusting a little faster, and she begins to move with me.

"God, you feel good," she says.

"And you feel even better," I respond.

I keep pumping into her, and she wraps her legs around me. And we continue on like that till we're both moaning together, and cumming at the same time.

Afterwards, I hold her close to me and just listen to her breathe.

Ivy Rose Gianelli—my wife, and the one who gave meaning to my life and gave me the babies who mean so much to me. How could I ever love another woman in this way? The answer is that I can't.

"We should make some more babies," she whispers. "I want a big family—what I didn't have growing up."

"Your dad was crazy not to want you," I say. "And I still feel like going back to Chicago and screaming at him for not caring about what happened to you. But I'd do a lot more than scream. I'd pound him into the damn ground."

"It's ok," she says. "I only care about our family, and our future as a family. And that means a lot more babies, if you're willing to make them with me."

I laugh. "Of course, Ivy Rose. I am always ready to make another baby with you."

"Good," she says. "Let's work on it all night long."

THE END

About the Author

Simone Black lives in Chicago with her husband, and a couple cats. She loves reading and writing romance, and she can't wait to share her twisted little stories with you. So make sure to follow her on Amazon to be notified of her frequent new releases!

www.ingramcontent.com/pod-product-compliance
Lightning Source LLC
Chambersburg PA
CBHW071449150726
48000CB00006B/2489